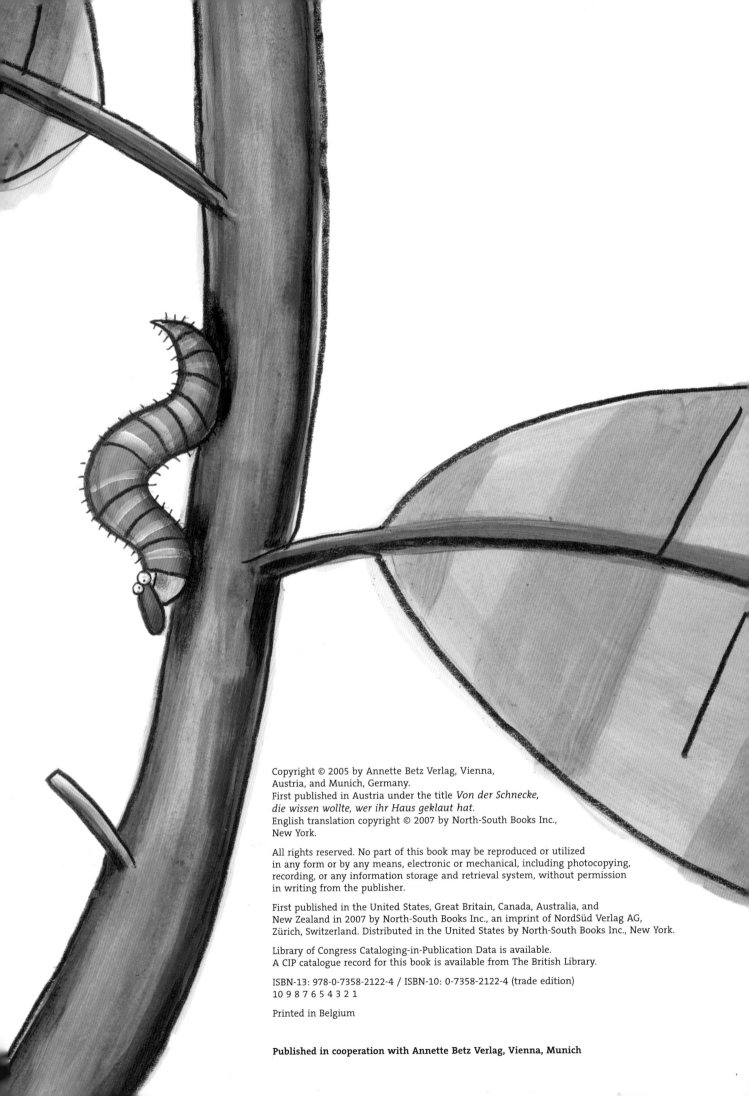

Copyright © 2005 by Annette Betz Verlag, Vienna,
Austria, and Munich, Germany.
First published in Austria under the title *Von der Schnecke,
die wissen wollte, wer ihr Haus geklaut hat.*
English translation copyright © 2007 by North-South Books Inc.,
New York.

First published in the United States, Great Britain, Canada, Australia, and
New Zealand in 2007 by North-South Books Inc., an imprint of NordSüd Verlag AG,
Zürich, Switzerland. Distributed in the United States by North-South Books Inc., New York.

Library of Congress Cataloging-in-Publication Data is available.
A CIP catalogue record for this book is available from The British Library.

ISBN-13: 978-0-7358-2122-4 / ISBN-10: 0-7358-2122-4 (trade edition)
10 9 8 7 6 5 4 3 2 1

Printed in Belgium

Published in cooperation with Annette Betz Verlag, Vienna, Munich

Who Stole My House?

By Barbara Veit
Illustrated by Anna Laura Cantone

Translated by Marianne Martens

NORTHSOUTH BOOKS
New York / London

Once upon a time, there was a little snail who had the nicest little house you've ever seen. One day, she decided to take a bath. She slipped out of her wonderful little house, tucked it under a leaf, and took a dewdrop bath.

Just as she was about to slip back into her house, something terrible happened. There was nothing under the leaf! Her beautiful snail house was gone!

"Help!" cried the little snail. "There are thieves and robbers on the loose!"

No one heard her except for a tiny ant.

"What happened?" he asked.

"Did you take my beautiful house?" asked the snail excitedly.

The ant thought for a while and then shook his head. "Who would steal a snail's house?" he murmured.

"Maybe some ants!" shouted the snail. "Ants are always carrying off stuff."

"Don't be silly," snapped the ant, who was feeling a little insulted. "What would an ant need a snail house for? We have our own homes!" he said, standing by his anthill.

The snail crept on till she saw a bird flying around a tree. "Hello, bird!" said the little snail. "Did you steal my beautiful house?"

"Did not, did not, did not," peeped the bird. "I have a lovely nest of my own. Besides, with five baby birds to take care of, who has time for stealing anything?"

The snail crept on till she came to a mouse. "Hello, mouse!" said the little snail. "Did you steal my beautiful house?"
The mouse was so insulted her whiskers trembled.

"The only things I'd ever steal are cheese and bacon. What would I need a snail house for? I have my own cozy mouse hole. It has a bed and a closet and two secret passages."

The snail crept on till she came to a squirrel.
"Hello, squirrel!" said the little snail. "Did you steal my beautiful house?"

"Who, me?" squeaked the squirrel, swishing her bushy tail through the air so swiftly that the snail almost toppled over. "Why would I take your house? I have my own tree house. Besides, I'm too busy gathering nuts to steal other people's houses."

The little snail crept on till she came to a *BIG* spider. The spider was
dangling on a long thread of web, swinging from a branch.

"Hello, spider," said the little snail. "Did you steal my beautiful house?"

"Well that's a very rude question," whispered the spider, because she couldn't talk any louder. "I'd never steal anything. I'm busy catching flies. What would I need your house for when I live in the finest web in the world? Mind you don't get stuck in it on your way out—snails are ever so sticky."

The snail crept on till she came to a dog. The dog almost didn't see her because she was so small. The snail had to yell to be heard. "Hello, dog!" shouted the little snail. "Did you steal my beautiful house?"

The dog cocked his head to one side and growled. "Hey, look here! I'm a watchdog. My job is to make sure that nothing gets stolen. Besides I have my own home," he said, poking his head through the door of his house.

It didn't look like she'd ever see her beautiful little house again. Sadly, the little snail crept on till she came to a bee. The bee buzzed about so wildly that the snail was afraid to even ask her. "Hello, bee, did you happen to see anyone stealing my house?"

The bee buzzed around the snail. "I see lots and lots of things, but unfortunately I haven't seen your house. Look at mine—I've just finished it. I've been working on it for weeks. I sure hope no one steals my house, but then again, my stinger will probably keep them away."

The snail went on till she came to a cow. She was *very* big. The snail gathered all her courage. "Hello, cow!" said the little snail. "Did you steal my beautiful house? Or maybe eat it?"

The cow chewed slowly from left to right and from right to left and,
after a long while, said, "Hmmmm, no. You should get a home like mine.
No one would ever steal or eat my house! It's much too big and heavy."

The little snail was feeling very discouraged, but kept on looking for her house. Instead of her house, she found a cat. "Hello, cat!" said the little snail. "Have you seen my beautiful house?"

"Haven't seen any snail houses," meowed the cat. "Just mice and bowls of milk. I have lots of homes of my own—the shed, the stall, the hayloft, and the house. My favorite one is the pillow by the stove."

It was getting late, and the little snail was getting cold. Still she crept on, and suddenly she saw something that looked like another snail only fatter and longer than she was. This snail also had no house.

"Hello, snail!" called the little snail. "Did someone steal your house, too?"

The slug waved her feelers and foamed a little. "What on earth are you talking about, you silly little snail? I'm a slug, not a snail."

"Snails carry houses on their backs, but slugs don't. That would give me a backache."

"But where do you live?" asked the little snail shyly.

"Under a flowerpot!" said the slug. "There's much more space there than in any old snail house."

The tired little snail was just about ready to ask if perhaps she could squeeze under the flowerpot, too . . .

But just then, under a dandelion leaf, she saw something that looked just like the most beautiful snail house in the world. She crept as quickly as she could. And there it was—her beautiful, and *not* stolen, snail house.

The little snail felt very silly. She had just looked under the wrong leaf after her bath! Her home had been there safe and sound the whole time! She rushed into her house and shut the door. She was so happy to be back home in the warmest, coziest, most *beautiful* house in the world.